ALICE IN WONDERLAND

A Dramatization of Lewis Carroll's "Alice's Adventures in Wonderland" and "Through the Looking Glass"

MAVEN BOOKS

ALICE IN WONDERLAND

A DRAMATIZATION OF LEWIS CARROLL'S "ALICE'S ADVENTURES IN WONDERLAND" AND "THROUGH THE LOOKING GLASS"

Lewis Carroll

&

Alice Gerstenberg

MAVEN BOOKS

Chennai　　　Trichy　　　Tirunelveli　　　New Delhi

An Imprint of **MJP Publishers**

ISBN 978-93-87867-35-2   **Maven Books**

All rights reserved   No. 44, Nallathambi Street,
Printed and bound in India   Triplicane, Chennai 600 005

MJP 552   © Publishers, 2018

Publisher : C. Janarthanan

Alice: You're Humpty Dumpty! Just like an egg.

TO THE MEMORY OF
LEWIS CARROLL

Introduction

This dramatic rendering of Alice in Wonderland, by Alice Gerstenberg of Chicago, was produced by The Players Producing Company of Chicago (Aline Barnsdall and Arthur Bissell), at the Fine Arts Theater, Chicago, February 11, 1915. After a successful run it opened at the Booth Theater, New York, March 23, 1915.

The scenery and the costumes were designed by William Penhallow Henderson of Chicago.

The music was written by Eric De Lamarter of Chicago.

The advertising posters and cards were designed by Jerome Blum of Chicago.

The illustrations of the characters of the play in this book were drawn by J. Allen St. John from photographs by Victor Georg of Chicago.

W. H. Gilmore staged the play with the following cast:

LEWIS CARROLL	Frank Stirling
ALICE	Vivian Tobin
RED QUEEN	Florence LeClercq
WHITE QUEEN	Mary Servoss
WHITE RABBIT	Donald Gallaher
HUMPTY DUMPTY	Alfred Donohoe
GRYPHON	Fred W. Permain
MOCK TURTLE	Geoffrey Stein
MAD HATTER	Geoffrey Stein
MARCH HARE	Fred W. Permain

DORMOUSE	J. Gunnis Davis
FROG FOOTMAN	Walter Kingsford
DUCHESS	Kenyon Bishop
CHESHIRE CAT	Alfred Donohoe
KING OF HEARTS	Frederick Annerly
QUEEN OF HEARTS	Winifred Hanley
KNAVE OF HEARTS	Foxhall Daingerfield
CATERPILLAR	Walter Kingsford
TWO OF SPADES	Rule Pyott
FIVE OF SPADES	France Bendtsen
SEVEN OF SPADES	John A. Rice

Contents

ACT I

Scene   I   Alice's Home   1

Scene   II   The Room in the Looking Glass   5

Scene III   The Hall with Doors   13

Scene IV   The Sea Shore   19

ACT II

Scene   I   The March Hare's Garden   27

ACT III

Scene   I   The Garden of Flowers   55

Scene   II   The Court of Hearts   65

Scene III   Alice's Home   75

ACT I

Scene One – Alice's Home

Lewis Carroll is discovered, playing chess. Golden-haired Alice, in a little blue dress, a black kitten in her arms, stands watching him.

ALICE: That's a funny game, uncle. What did you do then?

CARR.:   A red pawn took a white pawn; this way. You see, Alice, the chessboard is divided into sixty-four squares, red and white, and the white army tries to win and the red army tries to win. It's like a battle!

ALICE: With soldiers?

CARR.:   Yes, here are the Kings and Queens they are fighting for. That's the Red Queen and here's the White Queen.

ALICE: How funny they look!

CARR.:   See the crowns on their heads, and look at their big feet.

ALICE: It's a foot apiece, that's what it is! Do they hump along like this?

CARR.:   Here! You're spoiling the game. I must keep them all in their right squares.

ALICE: I want to be a queen!

CARR.:   Here *you* are [*he points to a small white pawn*] here *you* are in your little stiff skirt!

ALICE: How do you do, Alice!

CARR.:   And now you are going to move here.

ALICE: Let me move myself.

CARR.:   When you have traveled all along the board this
                way and haven't been taken by the enemy you may
                be a queen.

ALICE: Why do people always play with kings and queens?
                Mother has them in her playing cards too. Look!

*[ALICE goes to the mantel and takes a pack of playing cards from the
ledge.]*

                Here's the King of Hearts and here's his wife; she's
                the Queen of Hearts—isn't she cross-looking?
                wants to bite one's head off.

[CARROLL moves a pawn.]

                You're playing against yourself, aren't you?

CARR.:   That's one way of keeping in practice, Alice; I have
                friends in the university who want to beat me.

ALICE: But if you play against yourself I should think
                you'd want to cheat!

CARR.:   Does a nice little girl like you cheat when she plays
                against herself?

ALICE: Oh! I *never* do! I'd scold myself hard. I always
                pretend I'm *two* people too. It's lots of fun, isn't
                it? Sometimes when I'm all alone I walk up to the
                looking glass and talk to the other Alice. She's so
                silly, that Alice; she can't do anything by herself.
                She just mocks me all the time. When I laugh, she
                laughs, when I point my finger at her, she points
                her finger at me, and when I stick my tongue out
                at her she sticks her tongue out at me! Kitty has a
                twin too, haven't you darling?

[ALICE goes to the mirror to show Kitty her twin.]

CARR.:   I'll have to write a book some day about Alice—
                Alice in wonderland, "Child of the pure uncloud-
                ed brow and dreaming eyes of wonder!" or, Alice
                through the looking glass!

ALICE: Don't you wish sometimes you could go into look-
                   ing-glass house? See!

[ALICE *stands on an armchair and looks into the mirror.*]

                   There's the room you can see through the glass;
                   it's just the same as our living-room here, only the
                   things go the other way. I can see all of it—all but
                   the bit just behind the fireplace. Oh! I do wish
                   I could see that bit! I want so much to know if
                   they've a fire there. You never can tell, you know,
                   unless our fire smokes. Then smoke comes up in
                   that room too—but that may be just to make it
                   look as if they had a fire—just to pretend they had.
                   The books are something like our books, only the
                   words go the wrong way. Won't there ever be any
                   way of our getting through, uncle?

CARR.:   Do you think Kitty would find looking-glass milk
                   digestible?

ALICE: It doesn't sound awful good, does it; but I might
                   leave her at home. She's been into an awful lot
                   of mischief today. She found sister's knitting and
                   chased the ball all over the garden where sister was
                   playing croquet with the neighbors. And I ran and
                   ran after the naughty little thing until I was all out
                   of breath and so tired! I am tired.

[*She yawns and makes herself comfortable in the armchair.*]

CARR.:   [*Replaces the playing cards on the mantel and con-
                   sults his watch.*]

                   Take a nap. Yes, you have time before tea.

ALICE: [*Half asleep.*]

                   We're going to have mock turtle soup for supper!
                   I heard mamma tell the cook not to pepper it too
                   much.

CARR.:   What a funny little rabbit it is, nibbling all the
                   time!

[He leans gently over the back of her chair, and seeing[Pg 6] that she is going to sleep puts out the lamp light and leaves the room. A red glow from the fireplace illumines ALICE.*]*

[Dream music. A bluish light reveals the RED CHESS QUEEN *and the* WHITE CHESS QUEEN *in the mirror.]*

RED QUEEN: *[Points to* ALICE *and says in a mysterious voice.]*

There she is, let's call her over.

WHITE QUEEN: Do you think she'll come?

RED QUEEN: I'll call softly, Alice!

WHITE QUEEN: Hist, Alice.

RED QUEEN: Alice!

WHITE QUEEN: Hush—if she wakes and catches us—

BOTH QUEENS: Alice, come through into looking-glass house!

[Their hands beckon her.]

ALICE:

[Rises, and talks sleepily. The Queens disappear. ALICE *climbs from the arm of the chair to the back of another and so on up to the mantel ledge, where she picks her way daintily between the vases.]*

I—don't—know—how—I—can—get—through. I've tried—before—but the glass was hard—and I was afraid of cutting—my fingers—

[She feels the glass and is amazed to find it like gauze.]

Why, it's soft like gauze; it's turning into a sort of mist; why, it's easy to get through! Why—why— I'm going through!

[She disappears.]

Scene Two – The Room in the Looking Glass

[Is Scene One, reversed. The portieres are black and red squares like a chessboard. A soft radiance follows the characters mysteriously. As the curtain rises ALICE *comes through the looking glass; steps down, looks about in wonderment and goes to see if there is a "fire." The* RED QUEEN *rises out of the grate and faces her haughtily.]*

ALICE: Why, you're the Red Queen!

RED QUEEN: Of course I am! Where do you come from? And where are you going? Look up, speak nicely, and don't twiddle your fingers!

ALICE: I only wanted to see what the looking glass was like. Perhaps I've lost my way.

RED QUEEN: I don't know what you mean by your way; all the ways about here belong to *me*. Curtsey while you're thinking what to say. It saves time.

ALICE: I'll try it when I go home; the next time I'm a little late for dinner.

RED QUEEN: It's time for you to answer now; open your mouth a *little* wider when you speak, and always say, "Your Majesty." I suppose you don't want to lose your name?

ALICE: No, indeed.

RED QUEEN: And yet I don't know, only think how convenient it would be if you could manage to go home without it! For instance, if the governess wanted to call you to your lessons, she would call out "come here," and there she would have to leave off, because there wouldn't be any name for her to call, and of course you wouldn't have to go, you know.

ALICE:	That would never do, I'm sure; the governess would never think of excusing me from lessons for that. If she couldn't remember my name, she'd call me "Miss," as the servants do.
RED QUEEN:	Well, if she said "Miss," and didn't say anything more, of course you'd miss your lessons. I dare say you can't even read this book.
ALICE:	It's all in some language I don't know. Why, it's a looking-glass book, of course! And if I hold it up to a glass, the words will all go the right way again.

*J*ABBERWOCKY
'Twas brillig, and the slithy toves
Did gyre and gimble in the wabe;
All mimsy were the borogoves,
And the mome raths outgrabe.

	It seems very pretty, but it's rather hard to understand; somehow it seems to fill my head with ideas—only I don't exactly know what they are.
RED QUEEN:	I daresay you don't know your geography either. Look at the map!

[She takes a right angle course to the portieres and points to them with her sceptre.]

ALICE:	It's marked out just like a big chessboard. I wouldn't mind being a pawn, though of course I should like to be a Red Queen best.
RED QUEEN:	That's easily managed. When you get to the eighth square you'll be a Queen. It's a huge game of chess that's being played—all over the world. Come on, we've got to run. Faster, don't try to talk.
ALICE:	I can't.
RED QUEEN:	Faster, faster.
ALICE:	Are we nearly there?

RED QUEEN:	Nearly there! Why, we passed it ten minutes ago. Faster. You may rest a little now.
ALICE:	Why, I do believe we're in the same place. Everything's just as it was.

Alice: You're Humpty Dumpty! Just like an egg.

RED QUEEN:	Of course it is, what would you have it?
ALICE:	Well, in our country you'd generally get to somewhere else—if you ran very fast for a long time as we've been doing.
RED QUEEN:	A slow sort of country. Now *here* you see, it takes all the running *you* can do, to keep in the same place. If you want to get somewhere else, you must run at least twice as fast as that.
ALICE:	I'd rather not try, please! I'm quite content to stay here—only I *am* so hot and thirsty.
RED QUEEN:	I know what you'd like.

[*She takes a little box out of her pocket.*]

Have a biscuit?

[ALICE, *not liking to refuse, curtseys as she takes the biscuit and chokes.*]

RED QUEEN:	While you're refreshing yourself, I'll just take the measurements.

[*She takes a ribbon out of her pocket and measures the map with it.*]

At the end of two yards I shall give you your directions—have another biscuit?

ALICE: No thank you, one's *quite* enough.

RED QUEEN: Thirst quenched, I hope? At the end of three yards I shall repeat them—for fear of your forgetting them. At the end of *four*, I shall say good-bye. And at the end of five, I shall go! That Square belongs to Humpty Dumpty and that Square to the Gryphon and Mock Turtle and that Square to the Queen of Hearts. But you make no remark?

ALICE: I—I didn't know I had to make one—just then.

RED QUEEN: You *should* have said, "It's extremely kind of you to tell me all this," however, we'll suppose it said. Four! Good-bye! Five!

[RED QUEEN vanishes in a gust of wind behind the portieres. Rabbit music. WHITE RABBIT comes out of the fireplace and walks about the room hurriedly. He wears a checked coat, carries white kid gloves in one hand, a fan in the other and takes out his watch to look at it anxiously.]

WHITE RABBIT: Oh the Duchess! the Duchess! Oh! won't she be savage if I've kept her waiting!

ALICE: I've never seen a rabbit with a waistcoat and a watch! And a waistcoat pocket! If you please, sir—

WHITE RABBIT: Oh!

[He drops fan and gloves in fright and dashes out by way of the portieres in a gust of wind. ALICE picks up the fan and playfully puts on the gloves. The portieres flap in the breeze and a shawl flies in.]

ALICE:

[Catches the shawl and looks about for the owner; then meets the WHITE QUEEN.]

I'm very glad I happened to be in the way.

WHITE QUEEN:

[Runs in wildly, both arms stretched out wide as if she were flying, and cries in a helpless frightened way.]

Bread-and-butter, bread-and-butter.

ALICE: Am I addressing the White Queen?

WHITE QUEEN: Well, yes, if you call that a-dressing. It isn't my notion of the thing, at all.

ALICE: If your Majesty will only tell me the right way to begin, I'll do it as well as I can.

WHITE QUEEN: But I don't want it done at all. I've been a-dressing myself for the last two hours.

ALICE: Every single thing's crooked, and you're all over pins; may I put your shawl straight for you?

WHITE QUEEN: I don't know what's the matter with it! It's out of temper. I've pinned it here, and I've pinned it there, but there's no pleasing it.

ALICE: It *can't* go straight, you know, if you pin it all on one side, and dear me, what a state your hair is in!

WHITE QUEEN: The brush has got entangled in it! And I lost the comb yesterday.

ALICE:

[Takes out the brush and arranges the QUEEN'S *hair.]*

You look better now! But really you should have a lady's maid!

WHITE QUEEN: I'm sure I'll take you with pleasure. Two pence a week and jam every other day.

ALICE:

[Who cannot help laughing.]

I don't want you to hire me—and I don't care for jam.

WHITE QUEEN: It's very good jam.

ALICE: Well, I don't want any today, at any rate.

WHITE QUEEN: You couldn't have it if you *did* want it. The rule is, jam tomorrow and jam yesterday—but never jam today.

ALICE:	It must come sometimes to "jam today."
WHITE QUEEN:	No, it can't, it's jam every *other* day; today isn't any *other* day, you know.
ALICE:	I don't understand you, it's dreadfully confusing!
WHITE QUEEN:	That's the effect of living backwards, it always makes one a little giddy at first—
ALICE:	Living backwards! I never heard of such a thing!
WHITE QUEEN:	But there's one great advantage in it—that one's memory works both ways.
ALICE:	I'm sure *mine* only works one way. I can't remember things before they happen.
WHITE QUEEN:	It's a poor sort of memory that only works backwards.
ALICE:	What sort of things do you remember best?
WHITE QUEEN:	Oh, things that happened the week after next. For instance now:

[*She sticks a large piece of plaster on her finger.*]

	There's the King's messenger—he's in prison being punished; and the trial doesn't even begin till next Wednesday; and of course the crime comes last of all.
ALICE:	Suppose he never commits the crime?
WHITE QUEEN:	

[*Binding the plaster with ribbon.*]

	That would be all the better, wouldn't it?
ALICE:	Of course it would be all the better, but it wouldn't be all the better his being punished.
WHITE QUEEN:	You're wrong *there*, at any rate; were *you* ever punished?
ALICE:	Only for faults.
WHITE QUEEN:	And you were all the better for it, I know!

ALICE: Yes, but then I *had* done the things I was punished for; that makes all the difference.

WHITE QUEEN: But if you hadn't done them that would have been better still; better and better and better!

ALICE: There's a mistake somewhere—

WHITE QUEEN:

[Screams like an engine whistle, and shakes her hand.]

Oh, Oh, Oh! My finger's bleeding. Oh, Oh, Oh!

ALICE: What *is* the matter? Have you pricked your finger?

WHITE QUEEN: I haven't pricked it yet—but I soon shall—Oh, Oh, Oh!

ALICE: When do you expect to do it?

WHITE QUEEN: When I fasten my shawl again; the brooch will come undone directly. Oh, Oh!

[Brooch flies open and she clutches it wildly.]

ALICE: Take care! you're holding it all crooked!

WHITE QUEEN:

[Pricks her finger and smiles.]

That accounts for the bleeding, you see; now you understand the way things happen here.

ALICE: But why don't you scream now?

WHITE QUEEN: Why, I've done all the screaming already. What would be the good of having it all over again? Oh! it's time to run if you want to stay in the same place! Come on!

ALICE: No, no! Not so fast! I'm getting dizzy!!

WHITE QUEEN: Faster, faster!

ALICE: Everything's black before my eyes!

[There is music, and the sound of rushing wind, and in the darkness the WHITE QUEEN cries: "Faster, faster"; ALICE gasps: "I can't—please stop"; and the QUEEN replies: "Then you can't stay in the same place. I'll have to drop you behind. Faster—faster, good-bye."]

Scene Three – The Hall with Doors

When the curtain rises one sees nothing but odd black lanterns with orange lights, hanging, presumably, from the sky. The scene lights up slowly revealing ALICE *seated on two large cushions. She has been "dropped behind" by the* WHITE QUEEN *and is dazed to find herself in a strange hall with many peculiar doors and knobs too high to reach.*

ALICE:　　　　　Oh! my head! Where am I? Oh dear, Oh dear!

[She staggers up and to her amazement finds herself smaller than the table.]

　　　　　　　　I've never been smaller than any table before! I've always been able to reach the knobs! What a curious feeling. Oh! I'm shrinking. It's the fan—the gloves!

[She throws them away, feels her head and measures herself against table and doors.]

　　　　　　　　Oh! saved in time! But I never—never—

WHITE RABBIT:　Oh! my fan and gloves! Where *are* my—

ALICE:　　　　　Oh! Mr. Rabbit—please help me out—I want to go home—I want to go home—

WHITE RABBIT:　Oh! the Duchess! Oh! my fur and whiskers! She'll get me executed, as sure as ferrets are ferrets! Oh! *you* have them!

ALICE:　　　　　I'm sorry—you dropped them, you know—

WHITE RABBIT:

[Picks up fan and gloves and patters off.]

　　　　　　　　She'll chop off your head!

ALICE:　　　　　If you please sir—where am I?—won't you please— tell me how to get out—I want to get out—

WHITE RABBIT:

[Looking at his watch.]

Oh! my ears and whiskers, how late it's getting.

[A trap door gives way and RABBIT disappears. ALICE dashes after only in time to have the trap door bang in her face.]

ALICE:

[Amazed.]

It's a rabbit-hole—I'm small enough to fit it too! If I shrink any more it might end in my going out altogether like a candle. I wonder what I would be like then! What does the flame of a candle look like after the candle is blown out? I've never seen such a thing!

HUMPTY DUM.:

[Sits on the wall.]

Don't stand chattering to yourself like that, but tell me your name and your business.

ALICE: My *name* is Alice, but—

HUMPTY DUM.: It's a stupid name enough, what does it mean?

ALICE: *Must* a name mean something?

HUMPTY DUM.: Of course it must; *my* name means the shape I am—and a good, handsome shape it is, too. With a name like yours, you might be any shape, almost.

ALICE: You're Humpty Dumpty! Just like an egg.

HUMPTY DUM.: It's *very* provoking, to be called an egg—*very*.

ALICE: I said you *looked* like an egg, Sir, and some eggs are very pretty, you know.

HUMPTY DUM.: Some people have no more sense than a baby.

ALICE: Why do you sit here all alone?

HUMPTY DUM.: Why, because there's nobody with me. Did you think I didn't know the answer to *that*? Ask another.

ALICE: Don't you think you'd be safer down on the ground? That wall's so very narrow.

HUMPTY DUM.:   What tremendously easy riddles you ask! Of course I don't think so. Take a good look at me! I'm one that has spoken to a king, I am; to show you I'm not proud, you may shake hands with me!

[He leans forward to offer ALICE *his hand but she is too small to reach it.]*

                However, this conversation is going on a little too fast; let's go back to the last remark but one.

ALICE.:   I'm afraid I can't remember it.

HUMPTY DUM.:   In that case we start fresh, and it's my turn to choose a subject.

ALICE.:   You talk about it just as if it were a game.

HUMPTY DUM.:   So here's a question for you. How old did you say you were?

ALICE: Seven years and six months.

HUMPTY DUM.:   Wrong! You never said a word about it. Now if you'd asked *my* advice, I'd have said, "Leave off at seven—but—"

ALICE: I never ask advice about growing.

HUMPTY DUM.:   Too proud?

ALICE: What a beautiful belt you've got on. At least, a beautiful cravat, I should have said—no, a belt, I mean—I beg your pardon. If only I knew which was neck and which was waist.

HUMPTY DUM.:   It is a—*most—provoking*—thing, when a person doesn't know a cravat from a belt.

ALICE: I know it's very ignorant of me.

HUMPTY DUM.:   It's a cravat, child, and a beautiful one, as you say. There's glory for you.

ALICE: I don't know what you mean by "glory."

HUMPTY DUM.: When I use a word, it means just what I choose it to mean—neither more nor less.

ALICE: The question is, whether you *can* make words mean different things.

HUMPTY DUM.: The question is, which is to be master—that's all. Impenetrability! That's what I say!

ALICE: Would you tell me, please, what that means?

HUMPTY DUM.: I meant by "impenetrability" that we've had enough of that subject, and it would be just as well if you'd mention what you mean to do next, as I suppose you don't mean to stop here all the rest of **your life.**

ALICE: That's a great deal to make one word mean.

HUMPTY DUM.: When I make a word do a lot of work like that I always pay it extra.

ALICE: Oh!

HUMPTY DUM.: Ah, you should see 'em come round me of a Saturday night, for to get their wages, you know. That's all—Good-bye.

ALICE: Good-bye till we meet again.

HUMPTY DUM.: I shouldn't know you again, if we *did* meet, you're so exactly like other people.

ALICE: The face is what one goes by, generally.

HUMPTY DUM.: That's just what I complain of. Your face is the same as everybody has—the two eyes—so—nose in the middle, mouth under. It's always the same. Now if you had the two eyes on the same side of the nose, for instance—or the mouth at the top—that would be *some* help.

ALICE: It wouldn't look nice.

HUMPTY DUM.: Wait till you've tried! Good-bye.

[He disappears as he came.]

ALICE: Oh! I forgot to ask him how to—

[She tries to open the doors. They are all locked; she begins to weep. She walks weeping to a high glass table and sits down on its lower ledge. She sits on a big golden key and picks it up in surprise. She tries it on all the doors but it does not fit. She weeps and weeps—and Wonderland grows dark to her in her despair. In the darkness she cries, "Oh! I'm slipping! Oh, Oh! it's a lake; Oh! my tears! I'm floating!" A mysterious light shows a "Drink me" sign around a bottle on the top of the table. ALICE floats up to it panting, and holding on to the edge of the table takes up the bottle.]

ALICE: It isn't marked poison.

[She sips at it.]

This is good! Tastes like cherry tart, custard, pineapple, roast turkey, toffy and hot buttered toast— all together. Oh! Oh! I'm letting out like a telescope.

[A mysterious light shows her lengthening out.]

[Music.]

But the lake is rising too. Oh! Oh! it's deep! I'm drowning. Help, help, I'm drowning, I'm drowning in my tears!

GRYPHON: Hjckrrh. Hjckrrh!

[The GRYPHON, a huge green creature with big glittering wings, appears where HUMPTY DUMPTY had been and reaches glittering claws over to grab and save ALICE.]

Scene Four – The Sea Shore

Is symbolic of a wet and rocky shore in a weird green light. The MOCK
TURTLE *is weeping dismally.*

GRYPHON: Hjckrrh. Hjckrrh. Hjckrrh.

MOCK TURTLE:

[Answers with his weeping.]

GRYPHON:

[Drags ALICE *in.]*

                Drop your tears into the sea with his.

ALICE: He sobs as if he had a bone in his throat. He sighs
                as if his heart would break. What is his sorrow?

MOCK TURTLE: Oh, Gryphon, it's terrible!

GRYPHON: It's all his fancy that. Mock Turtle hasn't got no
                sorrow. This here young lady, she wants for to know
                your history, she do.

MOCK TURTLE: I'll tell it her. Sit down both of you, and don't speak
                a word till I've finished.

ALICE: I don't see how you can *ever* finish, if you don't
                begin.

MOCK TURTLE: Once, I was a real Turtle.

*[A long silence is broken only by the exclamations, "Hjckrrh," of
the* GRYPHON *and the heavy sobbing of the* MOCK TURTLE*.]*

MOCK TURTLE: When we were little, we went to school in the sea.
                The master was an old Turtle—we used to call him
                tortoise—

ALICE: Why did you call him Tortoise, if he wasn't one?

MOCK TURTLE: We called him Tortoise because he taught us; really you are very dull.

GRYPHON: You ought to be ashamed of yourself for asking such a simple question. Drive on, old fellow! Don't be all day about it!

MOCK TURTLE: Yes, we went to school in the sea, tho' you mayn't believe it—

ALICE: I never said I didn't.

MOCK TURTLE: You did.

GRYPHON: Hold your tongue!

MOCK TURTLE: We had the best of educations—in fact, we went to school every day.

ALICE: I've been to a day school too; you needn't be so proud as all that.

MOCK TURTLE: With extras?

ALICE: Yes, we learned French and music.

MOCK TURTLE: And washing?

ALICE: Certainly not!

MOCK TURTLE: Ah! Then yours wasn't a really good school. Now at *ours* they had at the end of the bill, French, music, *and washing*—extra.

ALICE: You couldn't have wanted it much; living at the bottom of the sea.

MOCK TURTLE: I couldn't afford to learn it, I only took the regular course.

ALICE: What was that?

MOCK TURTLE: Reeling and writhing, of course, to begin with, and then the different branches of Arithmetic—Ambition, Distraction, Uglification, and Derision.

ALICE: I never heard of Uglification. What is it?

GRYPHON: Never heard of uglifying! You know what to beautify is, I suppose?

ALICE: Yes, it means—to—make—anything—prettier.

GRYPHON: Well then, if you don't know what to uglify is, you *are* a simpleton.

ALICE: What else had you to learn?

MOCK TURTLE: Well, there was Mystery; Mystery, ancient and modern, with Seaography, then Drawling—the Drawling-master was an old conger eel, that used to come once a week; what *he* taught us was Drawling, Stretching, and Fainting in Coils.

ALICE: What was *that* like?

MOCK TURTLE: Well, I can't show it you, myself. I'm too stiff. And the Gryphon never learned it.

GRYPHON: Hadn't time; I went to the Classical master, though. He was an old crab, *he* was.

MOCK TURTLE: I never went to him; he taught Laughing and Grief, they used to say.

GRYPHON: So he did, so he did.

ALICE: And how many hours a day did you do lessons?

MOCK TURTLE: Ten hours the first day, nine the next, and so on.

ALICE: What a curious plan!

GRYPHON: That's the reason they're called lessons, because they lessen from day to day.

ALICE: Then the eleventh day must have been a holiday?

MOCK TURTLE: Of course it was.

ALICE: And how did you manage on the twelfth?

GRYPHON: That's enough about lessons, tell her something about the games now.

[MOCK TURTLE sighs deeply, draws back of one flapper across his eyes. He looks at ALICE and tries to speak but sobs choke his voice.]

GRYPHON:

[Punching him in the back.]

Same as if he had a bone in his throat.

MOCK TURTLE:

[With tears running down his cheeks.]

You may not have lived much under the sea—

ALICE: I haven't.

MOCK TURTLE: And perhaps you were never even introduced to a lobster.

ALICE: I once tasted—no, never!

MOCK TURTLE: So you can have no idea what a delightful thing a Lobster Quadrille is.

ALICE: No, indeed. What sort of a dance is it?

GRYPHON: Why, you first form into a line along the seashore.

MOCK TURTLE: Two lines; seals, turtles, salmon, and so on; then, when you've cleared all the jellyfish out of the way—

GRYPHON: *That* generally takes some time.

MOCK TURTLE: You advance twice—

GRYPHON: Each with a lobster as a partner.

MOCK TURTLE: Of course, advance twice, set to partners.

GRYPHON: Change lobsters, and retire in same order.

MOCK TURTLE: Then you know, you throw the—

GRYPHON: The lobsters!

MOCK TURTLE: As far out to sea as you can—

GRYPHON: Swim after them!

MOCK TURTLE: Turn a somersault in the sea.

GRYPHON: Change lobsters again!

MOCK TURTLE: Back to land again, and—that's all the first figure.

ALICE: It must be a very pretty dance.

MOCK TURTLE: Would you like to see a little of it?

ALICE: Very much indeed.

MOCK TURTLE: Come, let's try the first figure. We can do it without lobsters, you know; which shall sing?

GRYPHON: Oh, *you* sing, I've forgotten the words.

[Creatures solemnly dance round and round ALICE, *treading on her toes, waving fore-paws to mark time while* MOCK TURTLE *sings.]*

First Verse

"Will you walk a little faster!" said a whiting to a snail,
"There's a porpoise close behind us, and he's treading on my tail.
See how eagerly the lobsters and the turtles all advance!
They are waiting on the shingle—will you come and join the dance?
Will you, won't you, will you, won't you, will you join the dance?
Will you, won't you, will you, won't you, won't you join the dance?

Second Verse

"You can really have no notion how delightful it will be
When they take us up and throw us, with the lobsters, out to sea!"
But the snail replied, "Too far, too far!" and gave a look askance—
Said he thanked the whiting kindly, but he would not
join the dance.
Would not, could not, would not, could not,
would not join the dance.
Would not, could not, would not, could not,
could not join the dance.

[The creatures dance against ALICE, *pushing her back and forth between them. She protests and finally escapes; they bump against each other.]*

ALICE:	Thank you; it's a very interesting dance to watch, and I do so like that curious song about the whiting.
MOCK TURTLE:	Oh, as to the whiting, they—you've seen them, of course?
ALICE:	Yes, I've often seen them at din—

[Checks herself hastily.]

MOCK TURTLE:	I don't know where Din may be, but if you've seen them so often, of course you know what they're like.
ALICE:	I believe so, they have their tails in their mouths—and they're all over crumbs.
MOCK TURTLE:	You're wrong about the crumbs, crumbs would all wash off in the sea. But they *have* their tails in their mouths; and the reason is—

[MOCK TURTLE yawns and shuts his eyes.]

	Tell her about the reason and all that.
GRYPHON:	The reason is, that they *would* go with the lobsters to the dance. So they got thrown out to sea. So they had to fall a long way. So they got their tails fast in their mouths. So they couldn't get them out again. That's all.
ALICE:	Thank you, it's very interesting. I never knew so much about a whiting before.
GRYPHON:	I can tell you more than that, if you like. Do you know why it's called a whiting?
ALICE:	I never thought about it. Why?
GRYPHON:	It does the boots and shoes.
ALICE:	Does the boots and shoes!
GRYPHON:	Why, what are *your* shoes done with? I mean, what makes them so shiny?
ALICE:	They're done with blacking, I believe.

GRYPHON: Boots and shoes under the sea, are done with whiting. Now you know.

ALICE: And what are they made of?

GRYPHON: Soles and eels, of course; any shrimp could have told you that.

ALICE: If I'd been the whiting, I'd have said to the porpoise, "Keep back, please; we don't want *you* with us."

MOCK TURTLE: They were obliged to have him with them, no wise fish would go anywhere without a porpoise.

ALICE: Wouldn't it really?

MOCK TURTLE: Of course not; why if a fish came to me and told me he was going a journey, I should say, "With what porpoise?"

ALICE: Don't you mean purpose?

MOCK TURTLE: I mean what I say.

GRYPHON: Shall we try another figure of the Lobster Quadrille? Or would you like the Mock Turtle to sing you a song?

ALICE: Oh, a song please, if the Mock Turtle would be so kind.

GRYPHON: Um! No accounting for tastes! Sing her "Turtle Soup," will you, old fellow?

MOCK TURTLE:

[Sighs deeply and sometimes choked with sobs, sings.]

"Beautiful Soup, so rich and green,
Waiting in a hot tureen!
Who for such dainties would not stoop?
Soup of the evening, beautiful Soup!
Soup of the evening, beautiful Soup!
Beau—ootiful Soo—op,
Beau—ootiful Soo—oop,
Soo—oop of the e-e-evening,
Beautiful, beautiful Soup."

WHITE RABBIT:

[Enters, stretching out a red and white checked sash with which he separates ALICE *from the creatures.]*

Check!

MOCK TURTLE: They won't let her stay in our square.

WHITE RABBIT: The Queen is coming this way.

GRYPHON: She'll chop our heads off. Come on, come on, let's fly!

[The MOCK TURTLE *and* GRYPHON *grab* ALICE *and fly into the air.]*

CURTAIN

[The Curtain rises to reveal small silhouettes of the GRYPHON, MOCK TURTLE, *and* ALICE *in an orange-colored moon far away in the sky. Down below the* WHITE RABBIT *is shouting to them, "You'll be safe in the March Hare's garden."]*

ACT II

Scene One – The March Hare's Garden

The March Hare's garden, showing part of the Duchess' house. On a small platform there is a tea table, set with many cups, continuing into wings to give impression of limitless length. THE MARCH HARE, HATTER, and DORMOUSE are crowded at one end. ALICE sits on the ground where she has been dropped from the sky. Finding herself not bruised she rises and approaches the table.

MAR.HARE AND HAT.:

No room! No room!

ALICE.:   There's plenty of room!

[She sits in a large armchair at one end of the table.]

I don't know who you are.

MARCH HARE: I am the March Hare, that's the Hatter, and this is the Dormouse. Have some wine?

ALICE: I don't see any wine.

MARCH HARE: There isn't any.

ALICE: Then it wasn't very civil of you to offer it.

MARCH HARE: It wasn't very civil of you to sit down without being invited.

ALICE: I didn't know it was *your* table; it's laid for a great many more than three.

HATTER: Your hair wants cutting.

ALICE: You should learn not to make personal remarks; it's very rude.

HATTER: Why is a raven like a writing-desk?

ALICE:	Come, we shall have some fun now! I'm glad you've begun asking riddles—I believe I can guess that.
MARCH HARE:	So you mean that you think you can find out the answer to it?

HATTER:	Your hair wants cutting.
ALICE:	Exactly so.
MARCH HARE:	Then you should say what you mean.
ALICE:	I do; at least—at least I mean what I say—that's the same thing, you know.
HATTER:	Not the same thing a bit! Why, you might just as well say that "I see what I eat" is the same thing as, "I eat what I see!"
MARCH HARE:	You might just as well say that "I like what I get," is the same thing as "I get what I like."
DORMOUSE:	You might just as well say that "I breathe when I sleep" is the same thing as "I sleep when I breathe."
HATTER:	It *is* the same thing with you.

[Takes out his watch, looks at it uneasily, shakes it, holds it to his ear.]

	What day of the month is it?
ALICE:	The fourth.

HATTER: Two days wrong. I told you butter wouldn't suit the works!

MARCH HARE: It was the *best* butter.

HATTER: Yes, but some crumbs must have got in as well; you shouldn't have put it in with the bread-knife—

MARCH HARE:

[Takes the watch, looks at it gloomily, dips it into his cup of tea and looks at it again but doesn't know what else to say.]

It was the *best* butter, you know.

ALICE: What a funny watch! It tells the day of the month, and doesn't tell what o'clock it is.

HATTER: Why should it? Does *your* watch tell you what year it is?

ALICE: Of course not, but that's because it stays the same year for such a long time together.

HATTER: Which is just the case with *mine*.

ALICE: I don't quite understand you. What you said had no sort of meaning in it and yet it was certainly English.

HATTER:

[Pouring some hot tea on the DORMOUSE'S *nose.]*

The Dormouse is asleep again.

DORMOUSE: Of course, of course, just what I was going to remark myself.

HATTER: Have you guessed the riddle yet?

ALICE: No, I give it up, what's the answer?

HATTER: I haven't the slightest idea.

MARCH HARE: Nor I.

ALICE: I think you might do something better with the time, than wasting it in asking riddles that have no answers.

HATTER: If you knew Time as well as I do, you wouldn't talk about wasting *it*. It's *him*.

ALICE: I don't know what you mean.

HATTER: Of course you don't. I dare say you never even spoke to Time.

ALICE: Perhaps not, but I know I have to beat time when I learn music.

HATTER: Ah, that accounts for it. He won't stand beating. Now, if you only kept on good terms with him, he'd do almost anything you liked with the clock. For instance, suppose it were nine o'clock in the morning, just time to begin lessons. You'd only have to whisper a hint to Time, and round goes the clock in a twinkling! Half past one, time for dinner.

MARCH HARE: I only wish it was.

ALICE: That would be grand, certainly, but then—I shouldn't be hungry for it, you know.

HATTER: Not at first, perhaps, but you could keep it to half past one as long as you liked.

ALICE: Is that the way *you* manage?

HATTER: Not I, we quarreled last March—just before *he* went mad, you know. It was at the great concert given by the Queen of Hearts and I had to sing.

> *"Twinkle, twinkle, little bat!*
> *How I wonder what you're at!"*

You know the song, perhaps.

ALICE: I've heard something like it.

DORMOUSE: Twinkle, twinkle, twinkle—

HATTER: Well, I'd hardly finished the first verse when the Queen bawled out, "He's murdering the time! Off with his head!"

ALICE:	How dreadfully savage!
HATTER:	And ever since that, he won't do a thing I ask! It's always six o'clock now.
ALICE:	Is that the reason so many tea things are put out here?
HATTER:	Yes, that's it; it's always tea time, and we've no time to wash the things between whiles.
ALICE:	Then you keep moving round, I suppose?
HATTER:	Exactly so, as the things get used up.
ALICE:	But when you come to the beginning again?
MARCH HARE:	Suppose we change the subject. I vote the young lady tells us a story.
ALICE:	I'm afraid I don't know one.

MARCH HARE and HATTER:

> Then the Dormouse shall. Wake up Dormouse.

[They pinch him on both sides at once.]

DORMOUSE:

[Opens his eyes slowly and says in a hoarse, feeble voice.]

> I wasn't asleep, I heard every word you fellows were saying.

MARCH HARE:	Tell us a story.
ALICE:	Yes, please do!
HATTER:	And be quick about it, or you'll be asleep again before it's done.
DORMOUSE:	Once upon a time there were three little sisters, and their[Pg 56] names were Elsie, Lacie, and Tillie and they lived at the bottom of a well—
ALICE:	What did they live on?
DORMOUSE:	They lived on treacle.
ALICE:	They couldn't have done that, you know, they'd have been ill.

DORMOUSE:	So they were, *very* ill.
ALICE:	But why did they live at the bottom of a well?
MARCH HARE:	Take some more tea.
ALICE:	I've had nothing yet, so I can't take more.
HATTER:	You mean, you can't take *less*; it's very easy to take *more* than nothing.
ALICE:	Nobody asked *your* opinion.
HATTER:	Who's making personal remarks now?

ALICE:

[Helps herself to tea and bread and butter.]

   Why did they live at the bottom of a well?

DORMOUSE:

[Takes a minute or two to think.]

   It was a treacle-well.

ALICE:	There's no such thing!

HATTER and MARCH HARE:

   Sh! Sh!

DORMOUSE:	If you can't be civil, you'd better finish the story for yourself.

ALICE:

[Very humbly.]

No, please go on. I won't interrupt you again. I dare say there may be *one*.

DORMOUSE: One, indeed! And so these three little sisters—they were learning to draw, you know—

ALICE: What did they draw?

DORMOUSE: Treacle.

HATTER: I want a clean cup. Let's all move one place on.

[*HATTER moves on,* DORMOUSE *takes his place,* MARCH HARE *takes* DORMOUSE's *place and* ALICE *unwillingly takes* MARCH HARE's *place.*]

ALICE: I'm worse off than I was before. You've upset the milk jug into your plate.

MARCH HARE: It wasn't very civil of you to sit down without being invited.

ALICE: Where did they draw the treacle from?

HATTER: You can draw water out of a water well, so I should think you could draw treacle out of a treacle well—eh, stupid?

ALICE: But they were *in* the well.

DORMOUSE: Of course they were—well in. They were learning to draw, and they drew all manner of things—everything that begins with an M—

ALICE: Why with an M?

MARCH HARE: Why not?

[ALICE is silent and confused. HATTER pinches DORMOUSE to wake him up.]

DORMOUSE: *[Wakes with a little shriek and continues.]*

—that begins with an M, such as mousetraps and the moon and memory and muchness—you know you say things are "much of a muchness"—did you ever see such a thing as a drawing of a muchness?

HATTER: Did you?

ALICE: Really now you ask me, I don't think—

HATTER: Then you shouldn't talk.

MARCH HARE: No!

ALICE:

[Rises and walks away.]

You are very rude. It's the stupidest tea party I ever was at in all my life—

[WHITE RABBIT enters carrying a huge envelope with a seal and crown on it.]

MARCH HARE **and** HATTER:

No room! no room!

[Rabbit pays no attention to them but goes to the house and raps loudly. A footman in livery with a round face and large eyes like a frog and powdered hair opens the door.]

WHITE RABBIT: For the Duchess. An invitation from the Queen to play croquet.

FROG: From the Queen. An invitation for the Duchess to play croquet.

[WHITE RABBIT bows and goes out.]

MARCH HARE **and** HATTER:

[To WHITE RABBIT.]

No room! No room! No room!

[The Frog *disappears into the house but leaves the door open. There is a terrible din and many sauce pans fly out.]*

MARCH HARE: She's at it again.

HATTER: It's perfectly disgusting.

MARCH HARE: Let's move on.

[The platform moves off with table, chairs, MARCH HARE, *[Pg 63]* HATTER, *and* DORMOUSE. *Meanwhile the* FROG *has come out again and is sitting near the closed door, staring stupidly at the sky.* ALICE *goes to the door timidly and knocks.]*

FROG: There's no sort of use in knocking, and that for two reasons: first, because I'm on the same side of the door as you are; secondly, because they're making such a noise inside, no one could possibly hear you.

ALICE: Please then, how am I to get in?

FROG: There might be some sense in your knocking if we had the door between us. For instance, if you were *inside*, you might knock, and I could let you out, you know.

ALICE: How am I to get in?

FROG: I shall sit here, till tomorrow.

[The door opens and a large plate skims out straight at the FROG's *head; it grazes his nose and breaks into pieces.]*

*[*FROG *acts as if nothing had happened.]*

Or next day, maybe.

ALICE: How am I to get in?

FROG: *Are* you to get in at all? That's the first question, you know.

ALICE: It's really dreadful the way all you creatures argue. It's enough to drive one crazy.

FROG: I shall sit here, on and off, for days and days.

ALICE: But what am I to do?

FROG: Anything you like.

[He begins to whistle.]

ALICE: Where's the servant whose business it is to an-
                  swer the door?

FROG: Which door?

ALICE: *This* door, of course!

*[The FROG looks at the door, and rubs his thumb on it to see if the
paint will come off.]*

FROG: I shall sit here till tomorrow.

FROG: To answer the door? What's it been asking for?

ALICE: I don't know what you mean.

FROG: I speaks English, doesn't I? Or are you deaf?
                  What did it ask you?

ALICE: Nothing! I've been knocking at it.

FROG: Shouldn't do that—shouldn't do that, vexes it,
                  you know.

[He kicks the door.]

You let *it* alone, and it'll let *you* alone, you know.

ALICE: Oh, there's no use talking to you—

[She starts to open the door just as the DUCHESS comes out carrying a pig in baby's clothes. She sneezes—FROG sneezes and ALICE sneezes.]

DUCHESS: If everybody minded her own business—

[She sneezes.]

ALICE: It's pepper.

DUCHESS: Of course, my cook puts it in the soup.

ALICE: There's certainly too much pepper in the soup.

DUCHESS: Sneeze then and get rid of it!

[DUCHESS begins to sing to the baby, giving it a violent shake at the end of every line of the lullaby.]

> *"Speak roughly to your little boy,*
> *And beat him when he sneezes;*

[FROG and ALICE sneeze.]

> *He only does it to annoy,*
> *Because he knows it teases.*

[DUCHESS sneezes, FROG sneezes, ALICE sneezes.]

> *I speak severely to my boy,*
> *I beat him when he sneezes;*

[FROG sneezes, ALICE sneezes.]

> *For he can thoroughly enjoy*
> *The pepper when he pleases!"*

[DUCHESS sneezes, FROG sneezes, ALICE sneezes, DUCHESS gasps and gives a tremendous sneeze.]

ALICE: Oh dear!

[She jumps aside as kettles and pots come flying out of the door. The DUCHESS pays no attention.]

What a cook to have!

[She calls inside.]

Oh! *please* mind what you're doing!

[Another pan comes out and almost hits the baby.]

Oh! there goes his *precious* nose!

DUCHESS: If everybody minded her own business, the world would go round a deal faster than it does.

ALICE: Which would not be an advantage. Just think what work it would make with the day and night! You see the earth takes twenty-four hours to turn round on its axis—

DUCHESS: Talking of axes, chop off her head!

[The head of a grinning Cheshire cat appears in a tree above a wall.]

ALICE: Oh, what's that?

DUCHESS: Cat, of course.

ALICE: Why does it grin like that?

DUCHESS: It's a Cheshire cat! and that's why. *[To baby.]* Pig!

DUCHESS: I speak severely to my boy,
I beat him when he sneezes.

ALICE: I didn't know that Cheshire cats always grinned; in fact, I didn't know that cats *could* grin.

DUCHESS: They all can and most of 'em do.

ALICE: I don't know of any that do.

DUCHESS: You don't know much and that's a fact. Here, you may nurse it a bit, if you like!

[*Flings the baby at* ALICE.]

I must go and get ready to play croquet with the Queen.

[*She goes into the house.*]

ALICE: If I don't take this child away with me, they're sure to kill it in a day or two. Cheshire Puss, would you tell me please, which way I ought to walk from here?

CAT: That depends a good deal on where you want to get to.

ALICE: I don't much care where—

CAT: Then it doesn't matter which way you walk.

ALICE: So long as I get *somewhere*.

CAT: Oh, you're sure to do that, if you only walk long enough.

ALICE: Please, will you tell me what sort of people live about here?

CAT: All mad people.

ALICE: But I don't want to go among mad people.

CAT: Oh, you can't help that; we're all mad here. I'm mad. He's mad. He's dreaming now, and what do you think he's dreaming about?

ALICE:

[*Goes to the* FROG *to scrutinize his face.*]

Nobody could guess that.

CAT: Why, about you! And if he left off dreaming about you, where do you suppose you'd be?

ALICE: Where I am now, of course.

CAT:	Not you. You'd be nowhere. Why, you're only a sort of thing in his dream; and you're mad too.
ALICE:	How do you know I'm mad?
CAT:	You must be, or you wouldn't have come here.
ALICE:	How do you know that you're mad?
CAT:	To begin with, a dog's not mad. You grant that?
ALICE:	I suppose so.
CAT:	Well then, you see a dog growls when it's angry, and wags its[Pg 72] tail when it's pleased. Now I growl when I'm pleased, and wag my tail when I'm angry. Therefore I'm mad.
ALICE:	I call it purring, not growling.

CAT:	Call it what you like. Do you play croquet with the Queen today?
ALICE:	I should like it very much, but I haven't been invited yet.
CAT:	You'll see me there.

[Vanishes.]

ALICE:

[To squirming baby.]

Oh, dear, it's heavy and so ugly. Don't grunt—Oh—Oh—it's a—pig. Please Mr. Footman take it!

FROG:

[Rises with dignity, whistles and disappears into the house; a kettle comes bounding out. ALICE puts pig down and it crawls off.]

CAT:

[Appearing again.]

By-the-bye, what became of the baby?

ALICE: It turned into a pig.

CAT: I thought it would.

[Vanishes.]

[FROG comes out of the house with hedgehogs and flamingoes.]

CAT:

[Reappearing.]

Did you say pig, or fig?

ALICE: I said pig; and I wish you wouldn't keep appearing and vanishing so suddenly; you make one quite giddy.

CAT: All right. *[It vanishes slowly.]*

[FROG puts flamingoes down and reenters house. While ALICE is examining the flamingoes curiously, TWEEDLEDUM and TWEEDLEDEE, each with an arm round the other's neck, sidestep in and stand looking at ALICE.]

ALICE:

[Turns, sees them, starts in surprise and involuntarily whispers.]

Tweedle—dee.

DUM: Dum!

DEE: If you think we're waxworks, you ought to pay.

DUM: Contrariwise, if you think we're alive, you ought to speak.

DEE: The first thing in a visit is to say "How d'ye do?" and shake hands!

[The brothers give each other a hug, then hold out the two hands that are free, to shake hands with her. ALICE does not like shaking hands with either of them first, for fear of hurting the other one's feelings; she takes hold of both hands at once and they all dance round in a ring, quite naturally to music, "Here we go round the mulberry bush."]

ALICE: Would you tell me which road leads out of—

DEE: What shall I repeat to her?

DUM: The "Walrus and the Carpenter" is the longest.

[Gives his brother an affectionate hug.]

DEE: The sun was shining—

ALICE: If it's very long, would you please tell me first which road—

DEE: The moon was shining sulkily.

DUM: The sea was wet as wet could be—

DEE:

> *O Oysters, come and walk with us*
> *The Walrus did beseech—*

DUM:

[Looks at DEE.]

> *A pleasant walk, a pleasant talk,*
> *Along the briny beach—*

DEE:

[Looks at DUM.]

> *The eldest Oyster winked his eye*
> *And shook his heavy head—*

DUM:

[Looks at DEE.]

> *Meaning to say he did not choose*
> *To leave the oyster bed.*

Dee:

> *But four young Oysters hurried up*
> *And yet another four—*

Dum:

> *And thick and fast they came at last,*
> *And more, and more, and more—*

Dee:

> *The Walrus and the Carpenter*
> *Walked on a mile or so,*

Dum:

> *And then they rested on a rock*
> *Conveniently low,*

Dee:

> *And all the little Oysters stood*
> *And waited in a row.*

Dum:

> *"A loaf of bread," the Walrus said,*
> *"Is what we chiefly need.*

Dee:

> *Now if you're ready, Oysters dear,*
> *We can begin to feed."*

Dum:

> *"But not on us!" the Oysters cried,*
> *Turning a little blue.*

Dee:

> *"The night is fine," the Walrus said,*
> *"Do you admire the view?"*

DUM:

> *The Carpenter said nothing but*
> *"Cut us another slice.*
> *I wish you were not quite so deaf—*
> *I've had to ask you twice!"*

DEE:

> *"It seems a shame," the Walrus said,*
> *"To play them such a trick,*
> *After we've brought them out so far,*
> *And made them trot so quick!"*

DUM:

> *"O, Oysters," said the Carpenter,*
> *"You've had a pleasant run!*

DEE: Shall we be trotting home again?"

DUM: But answer came there none—

DEE: And this was scarcely odd, because

DUM: They'd eaten every—

DEE:

[Interrupts in a passion, pointing to a white rattle on the ground.]

Do you see *that?*

ALICE: It's only a rattle—

DUM:

[Stamps wildly and tears his hair.]

I knew it was! It's spoilt of course. My nice new rattle!

[To DEE.]

You agree to have a battle?

[He collects sauce pans and pots.]

DEE:

[Picks up a sauce pan.]

I suppose so. Let's fight till dinner.

[They go out hand in hand.]

ALICE:

[Hears music.]

I wonder what is going to happen next.

[She backs down stage respectfully as the KING *and* QUEEN OF HEARTS *enter, followed by the* KNAVE OF HEARTS *carrying the* KING'S *crown on a crimson velvet cushion, and the* WHITE RABBIT *and others. When they come opposite to* ALICE *they stop and look at her.]*

[The DUCHESS *comes out of her house.]*

QUEEN:

[To the KNAVE.*]*

Who is this?

KNAVE:

[Bows three times, smiles and giggles.]

QUEEN:	Idiot! What's your name, child?
ALICE:	My name is Alice, so please your Majesty.
QUEEN:	Off with her head! Off—
ALICE:	Nonsense!
KING:	Consider, my dear, she is only a child.
QUEEN:	Can you play croquet?
ALICE:	Yes.
QUEEN:	Come on then. Get to your places. Where are the mallets?
DUCHESS:	Here.

[The FROG *appears with the flamingoes and hedgehogs.]*

QUEEN:	Off with his head!

[No one pays any attention.]

KNAVE:	What fun!

ALICE:	What is the fun?
KNAVE:	Why she; it's all her fancy, that. They never execute anyone.
ALICE:	What does one do?
QUEEN:	Get to your places!

[She takes a flamingo, uses its neck as a mallet and a hedgehog as a ball. The FROG doubles himself into an arch. The KING does the same with the followers and the KNAVE offers himself as an arch for AL-ICE. Even though ALICE does not notice him he holds the arch position. The QUEEN shouts at intervals, "Off with his head, off with her head."]

ALICE:	Where are the Chess Queens?
RABBIT:	Under sentence of execution.
ALICE:	What for?
RABBIT:	Did you say, "what a pity"?
ALICE:	No, I didn't. I don't think it's at all a pity. I said, "What for?"
RABBIT:	They boxed the Queen's ears.

[ALICE gives a little scream of laughter.]

RABBIT:	Oh, hush! The Queen will hear you! You see they came rather late and the Queen said—Oh dear, the Queen hears me—

[He hurries away.]

ALICE:

[Noticing the KNAVE who still pretends to be an arch.]

	How *can* you go on thinking so quietly, with your head downwards?
KNAVE:	What does it matter where my body happens to be? My mind goes on working just the same. The fact of it is, the more head downwards I am, the more I keep on inventing new things.

KING:	Did you happen to meet any soldiers, my dear, as you came through the wood?
ALICE:	Yes, I did; several thousand I should think.
KING:	Four thousand, two hundred and seven, that's the exact number. They couldn't send all the horses, you know, because two of them are wanted in the game. And I haven't sent the two messengers, either.
ALICE:	What's the war about?
KING:	The red Chess King has the whole army against us but he can't kill a man who has thirteen hearts.

[The DUCHESS, QUEEN, FROG, *and followers go out. The* KNAVE *and the* FIVE-SPOT, SEVEN-SPOT, *and* NINE-SPOT OF HEARTS *stand behind the* KING.*]*

KING:	I only wish I had such eyes; to be able to see Nobody!
KING:	Just look along the road and tell me if you can see either of my messengers.
ALICE:	I see nobody on the road.
KING:	I only wish I had such eyes; to be able to see Nobody! And at that distance too! Why, it's as much as I can do to see real people, by this light.
ALICE:	I see somebody now! But he's coming very slowly—and what curious attitudes he goes into—skipping up and down, and wriggling like an eel.

KING: Not at all, those are Anglo-Saxon attitudes. He only does them when he's happy. I must have two messengers, you know—to come and go. One to come and one to go.

ALICE: I beg your pardon?

KING: It isn't respectable to beg.

ALICE: I only meant that I didn't understand. Why one to come and one to go?

KING: Don't I tell you? I must have two—to fetch and carry. One to fetch, and one to carry.

MARCH HARE:

[Enters, pants for breath—waves his hands about and makes fearful faces at the KING.*]*

KING: You alarm me! I feel faint—give me a ham sandwich. Another sandwich!

MARCH HARE: There's nothing but hay left now.

KING: Hay, then. There's nothing like eating hay when you're faint.

ALICE: I should think throwing cold water over you would be better.

KING: I didn't say there was nothing *better*; I said there was nothing *like* it.

KING: Who did you pass on the road?

MARCH HARE: Nobody.

KING: Quite right; this young lady saw him too. So of course Nobody walks slower than you.

MARCH HARE: I do my best; I'm sure nobody walks much faster than I do.

KING: He can't do that; or else he'd have been here first. However, now you've got your breath, you may tell us what's happened in the town.

MARCH HARE: I'll whisper it.

[Much to ALICE'S *surprise, he shouts into the* KING'S *ear.]*

They're at it again!

KING: Do you call *that* a whisper? If you do such a thing again, I'll have you buttered. It went through and through my head like an earthquake. Give me details, quick!

[The KING *and* MARCH HARE *go out, followed by* FIVE, SEVEN, *and* NINE SPOTS.]*

DUCHESS:

[Runs in and tucks her arm affectionately into ALICE'S.]*

You can't think how glad I am to see you again, you dear old thing!

ALICE: Oh!

DUCHESS: You're thinking about something, my dear, and that makes you forget to talk. I can't tell you just now what the moral of that is, but I shall remember it in a bit.

ALICE: Perhaps it hasn't one.

DUCHESS: Tut, tut, child! Everything's got a moral, if only you can find it.

[Squeezes closely, digs her chin into ALICE'S *shoulder, and roughly drags* ALICE *along for a walk.]*

ALICE: The game's going on rather better now.

DUCHESS: 'Tis so, and the moral of that is—"Oh, 'tis love, 'tis love, that makes the world go round!"

ALICE: Somebody said, that it's done by everybody minding their own business.

DUCHESS: Ah, well! It means much the same thing, and the moral of *that* is—"Take care of the sense, and the sounds will take care of themselves."

ALICE: How fond you are of finding morals in things.

DUCHESS: I daresay you're wondering why I don't put my arm round your waist. The reason is, that I'm doubtful about the temper of your flamingo. Shall I try the experiment?

ALICE: He might bite.

DUCHESS: Very true; flamingoes and mustard both bite. And the moral of that is—"Birds of a feather flock together."

ALICE: Only mustard isn't a bird.

DUCHESS: Right, as usual; what a clear way you have of putting things.

ALICE: It's a mineral, I *think*.

DUCHESS: Of course it is; there's a large mustard mine near here. And the moral of that is—"The more there is of mine, the less there is of yours."

ALICE: Oh! I know, it's a vegetable. It doesn't look like one, but it is.

DUCHESS: I quite agree with you, and the moral of that is—"Be what you would seem to be;" or, if you'd like it put more simply, "Never imagine yourself not to be otherwise than what it might appear to others that what you were or might have been was not otherwise than what you had been would have appeared to them to be otherwise."

ALICE: I think I should understand that better if I had it written down, but I can't quite follow it as you say it.

DUCHESS: That's nothing to what I could say if I chose.

ALICE: Pray don't trouble yourself to say it any longer than that.

DUCHESS: Oh, don't talk about trouble; I make you a present of everything I've said as yet.

ALICE: Uhm!

DUCHESS: Thinking again?

ALICE: I've got a right to think.

DUCHESS: Just about as much right as pigs have to fly, and the moral—

[The arm of the DUCHESS begins to tremble and her voice dies down. The QUEEN OF HEARTS stands before them with folded arms and frowning like a thunderstorm.]

DUCHESS: A fine day, your Majesty.

QUEEN: Now, I give you fair warning, either you or your head must be off, and that in about half no time. Take your choice!

[The DUCHESS goes meekly into the house.]

QUEEN: Let's go on with the game.

[She goes off and shouts at intervals, "Off with his head; off with her head."]

CAT: How are you getting on?

ALICE: It's no use speaking to you till your ears have come. I don't think they play at all fairly and they all quarrel so and they don't seem to have any rules in particular. And you've no idea how confusing it is with all the things alive; there's the arch I've got to go through next walking about at the other end of the ground—and I should have croqueted the Queen's hedgehog just now, only it ran away when it saw mine coming.

[Music begins.]

CAT: How do you like the Queen?

ALICE: Not at all; she's so extremely—

[The KING, QUEEN and entire court enter. The QUEEN is near to ALICE. The music stops and all look at ALICE questioningly.]

[ALICE tries to propitiate the QUEEN.]

—likely to win,

[Music continues.]

that it's hardly worth while finishing the game.

[QUEEN smiles and passes on.]

KING:	Who *are* you talking to?
ALICE:	It's a friend of mine—a Cheshire Cat—allow me to introduce it.
KING:	I don't like the look of it at all; however, it may kiss my hand if it likes.
CAT:	I'd rather not.
KING:	Don't be impertinent and don't look at me like that.
ALICE:	A cat may look at a king. I've read that in some book, but I don't remember where.
KING:	Well, it must be removed. My dear! I wish you would have this cat removed.
QUEEN:	Off with his head!
KNAVE:	But you can't cut off a head unless there's a body to cut it off from.
KING:	Anything that has a head can be beheaded.
QUEEN:	If something isn't done about it in less than no time, I'll have everybody executed, all round.
ALICE:	It belongs to the Duchess; you'd better ask her about it.
DUCHESS:	It's a lie!
CAT:	You'd better ask me. Do it if you can.

[It grins away. The DUCHESS and FROG escape into the house.]

QUEEN:	Cut it off!
KING:	It's gone.
EVERYBODY:	It's gone! It's gone! Where, where, where—

QUEEN: Cut it off. Cut them all off!

EVERYBODY: No, no, no!

ALICE: Save me, save me!

KNAVE:

[Shouts to ALICE *and gives her a tart for safety.]*

                Take a tart!

QUEEN:

[Seeing ALICE *stand out a moment from the others.]*

                Cut hers off! Cut hers off!

OTHERS:

[Glad to distract QUEEN'S *attention from themselves.]*

                Cut hers off, cut hers off, cut—

ALICE:

[Cries in fear and takes a quick bite at the tart. If there is a trap door on the stage ALICE *disappears down it, leaving the crowd circling around the hole screaming and amazed. If the stage has no trap door, a bridge is built across the footlights with stairs leading down into the orchestra pit. When the crowd is chasing* ALICE *she jumps over the footlights onto the bridge and as the curtain is falling dividing her from the crowd she appeals to the audience, "Save me, save me, who will save me?" and runs down the stairs and disappears.]*

— CURTAIN —

ACT III

Scene One – The Garden of Flowers

Is a garden of high, very conventional and artificial looking flowers. On a large mushroom sits the Caterpillar smoking a hookah. Alice is whirling about trying to get her equilibrium after her fall. She goes to the mushroom timidly and, conscious of her size, for her chin reaches the top of the mushroom, she gazes at the Caterpillar wonderingly. He looks at her lazily and speaks in a languid voice.

CATERPILLAR:	Who are you?
ALICE:	I—I hardly know, sir, just at present. The Queen frightened me so and I've had an awfully funny fall down a tunnel or a sort of well. At least I know who I was when I got up this morning, but I think I must have been changed several times since then.
CATERPILLAR:	What do you mean by that? Explain yourself.
ALICE:	I can't explain myself, I'm afraid, Sir, because I'm not myself, you see. Being so many different sizes in a day is very confusing.

CATERPILLAR:	You! Who are you?
ALICE:	I think you ought to tell me who you are, first.
CATERPILLAR:	Why?

[As Alice turns away.]

Come back. I've something important to say.

[Alice comes back.]

Keep your temper.

ALICE: Is that all?

CATERPILLAR: No.

[He puffs at the hookah in silence; finally takes it out of his mouth and unfolds his arms.]

So you think you're changed, do you?

ALICE: I'm afraid I am, Sir; I don't keep the same size.

CATERPILLAR: What size do you want to be?

ALICE: I don't know. At least I've never been so small as a caterpillar.

CATERPILLAR:

[Rears angrily.]

It is a very good height indeed.

ALICE: But I'm not used to it; I wish you wouldn't all be so easily offended.

CATERPILLAR: You'll get used to it in time.

ALICE: Are you too big or am I too small?

[She compares her height wonderingly with the tall flowers.]

CATERPILLAR:

[Looks at her sleepily, yawns, shakes himself, slides down from the mushroom and crawls slowly away.]

One side will make you grow taller, and the other side will make you grow shorter.

ALICE: One side of what? The other side of what?

CATERPILLAR: Of the mushroom.

[ALICE hesitates, then embraces mushroom and picks bit from each side.]

[Three gardeners representing spades enter carrying brushes and red paint cans.]

TWO-SPOT: Look out now, Five. Don't go splashing paint over me like that.

FIVE-SPOT: I couldn't help it. Seven jogged my elbow.

SEVEN-SPOT: That's right, Five, always lay the blame on others.

FIVE-SPOT: You'd better not talk. I heard the Queen say only yesterday you deserved to be beheaded.

TWO-SPOT: What for?

SEVEN-SPOT: That's none of your business, Two.

FIVE-SPOT: Yes, it is his business, and I'll tell him. It was for bringing the cook tulip roots instead of onions.

SEVEN-SPOT: Well, of all the unjust things—

[*Sees* ALICE; *others look around, all bow.*]

ALICE: Could you please tell me what side to eat?

[FIVE *and* SEVEN *look at* TWO.]

TWO-SPOT: I don't know anything about it.

[*He paints a white rose, red.*]

              You ought to have been red, we put you in by mistake, and if the Queen was to find it out we should all have our heads cut off.

[*A thumping is heard off stage and the music grows louder and louder.*]

ALICE: What's that?

FIVE-SPOT: The White Chess Queen.

SEVEN-SPOT: Don't let her see what we are doing.

TWO-SPOT: She'll tell on us.

SEVEN-SPOT: Run out and stop her from coming here.

FIVE-SPOT:

[*To* ALICE *as she runs to the right.*]

              No, no, the other way.

ALICE: But she's off there!

Two-Spot: You can only meet her by walking the other way.

Alice: Oh! what nonsense.

All the Gardeners:

                   Go the other way!

Alice:

[Re-enters in dismay and dashes out to the left.]

                   She's running away from me.

[The White Queen backs in from right and Alice backs in from left. They meet. The gardeners cry "The Queen" and throw themselves flat upon the ground; their backs are like the backs of the rest of the pack. Music stops. Alice looks at the Queen curiously.]

Alice: Oh, there you are! Why, I'm just the size I was when I saw you last.

White Queen: Of course you are, and who are these? I can't tell them by their backs.

[She turns them over with her foot.]

                   Turn over. Ah! I thought so! Get up! What have you been doing here?

Two-Spot: May it please your Majesty, we were trying—

White Queen:

[Examines rose.]

                   I see! Begone, or I'll send the horses after you, and tell the Queen of Hearts.

[Gardeners rush off. The Red Queen enters. Alice has gone to the mushroom again to look at its sides and there to her amazement finds a gold crown and scepter, which she immediately appropriates. Music. The Queens watch Alice superciliously. Alice puts on her crown, proudly exclaiming in great elation, "Queen Alice," and walks down stage bowing right and left to the homage of imaginary subjects. She repeats as if scarcely daring to believe it true, "Queen Alice." Music stops.]

RED QUEEN:	Ridiculous!
ALICE:	Isn't this the Eighth Square?
RED QUEEN:	You can't be a Queen, you know, till you've passed the proper examination.
WHITE QUEEN:	The sooner we begin it, the better.
ALICE:	Please, would you tell me—
RED QUEEN:	Speak when you're spoken to.
ALICE:	But if everybody obeyed that rule, and if you only spoke when you were spoken to, and the other person always waited for you to begin, you see nobody would ever say anything, so that—
RED QUEEN:	Preposterous.
ALICE:	I only said "if."
RED QUEEN:	She says she only said "if."

WHITE QUEEN:

[Moans and wrings her hands.]

But she said a great deal more than that. Ah, yes, so much more than that.

RED QUEEN:	So you did, you know; always speak the truth—think before you speak—and write it down afterwards.
ALICE:	I'm sure I didn't mean—
RED QUEEN:	That's just what I complained of. You *should* have meant! What do you suppose is the use of a child without any meaning? Even a joke should have some meaning—and a child's more important than a joke, I hope. You couldn't deny that, even if you tried with both hands.
ALICE:	I don't deny things with my *hands*.
RED QUEEN:	Nobody said you did. I said you couldn't if you tried.

WHITE QUEEN: She's in that state of mind, that she wants to deny *something*—only she doesn't know what to deny!

RED QUEEN: A nasty, vicious temper. I invite you to Alice's dinner party this afternoon.

WHITE QUEEN: And I invite *you*.

ALICE: I didn't know I was to have a party at all; but if there is to be one, I think I ought to invite the guests.

RED QUEEN: We gave you the opportunity of doing it, but I dare say you've not had many lessons in manners yet.

ALICE: Manners are not taught in lessons; lessons teach you to do sums, and things of that sort.

WHITE QUEEN: Can you do addition? What's one and one and one and one and one and one and one and one and one and one?

ALICE: I don't know. I lost count.

RED QUEEN: She can't do addition; can you do subtraction? Take nine from eight.

ALICE: Nine from eight I can't, you know, but—

WHITE QUEEN: She can't do subtraction. Can you do division? Divide a loaf by a knife—what's the answer to that?

ALICE: I suppose—

RED QUEEN:

[*Answers for her.*]

Bread and butter, of course. Try another subtraction sum. Take a bone from a dog; what remains?

ALICE: The bone wouldn't remain, of course, if I took it—and the dog wouldn't remain; it would come to bite me—and I'm sure I shouldn't remain.

RED QUEEN:	Then you think nothing would remain?
ALICE:	I think that's the answer.
RED QUEEN:	Wrong as usual; the dog's temper would remain.
ALICE:	But I don't see how—
RED QUEEN:	Why, look here; the dog would lose its temper, wouldn't it?
ALICE:	Perhaps it would.
RED QUEEN:	Then if the dog went away, its temper would remain!
ALICE:	They might go different ways! What dreadful nonsense we *are* talking.
BOTH QUEENS:	She can't do sums a bit!
ALICE:	Can *you* do sums?
WHITE QUEEN:	I can do addition, if you give me time—but I can't do *subtraction* under *any* circumstances.
RED QUEEN:	Of course you know your A, B, C?
ALICE:	To be sure I do.
WHITE QUEEN:	So do I; we'll often say it over together, dear. And I'll tell you a secret—I can read words of one letter. Isn't that grand? However, don't be discouraged. You'll come to it in time.
RED QUEEN:	Can you answer useful questions? How is bread made?
ALICE:	I know *that*! You take some flour—
WHITE QUEEN:	Where do you pick the flower? In a garden or in the hedges?
ALICE:	Well, it isn't *picked* at all. It's ground—
WHITE QUEEN:	How many acres of ground? You mustn't leave out so many things.
RED QUEEN:	Fan her head! She'll be feverish after so much thinking.

[They fan her with bunches of leaves which blow her hair wildly.]

ALICE: Please—please—

RED QUEEN: She's all right again now. Do you know languages? What's the French for fiddle-de-dee?

ALICE: Fiddle-de-dee's not English.

RED QUEEN: Who ever said it was?

ALICE: If you tell me what language fiddle-de-dee is, I'll tell you the French for it!

RED QUEEN: Queens never make bargains!

ALICE: I wish Queens never asked questions!

WHITE QUEEN: Don't let us quarrel; what is the cause of lightning?

ALICE: The cause of lightning is the thunder—no, no! I meant the other way.

RED QUEEN: It's too late to correct it; when you've once said a thing, that fixes it, and you must take the consequences.

WHITE QUEEN: We had *such* a thunderstorm next Tuesday, you can't think.

RED QUEEN: She *never* could, you know.

WHITE QUEEN: Part of the roof came off, and ever so much thunder got in—and it went rolling round the room in great lumps—and knocking over the tables and things—till I was so frightened, I couldn't remember my own name!

ALICE: I never should *try* to remember my name in the middle of an accident. Where would be the use of it?

RED QUEEN: You must excuse her. She means well, but she can't help saying foolish things, as a general rule. She never was really well brought up, but it's amazing how good tempered she is! Pat her on the head, and see how pleased she'll be! A little kindness and putting her hair in papers would do wonders with her.

WHITE QUEEN:

[Gives a deep sigh and leans her head on ALICE'S *shoulder.]*

I *am* so sleepy!

RED QUEEN: She's tired, poor thing; smooth her hair—lend her your night cap—and sing her a soothing lullaby.

ALICE: I haven't got a night cap with me, and I don't know any soothing lullabies.

ALICE: Do wake up, you heavy things!

RED QUEEN: I must do it myself, then.

Hush-a-by lady, in Alice's lap!
Till the feast's ready, we've time for a nap;
When the feast's over, we'll go to the ball—
Red Queen and White Queen and Alice and all!

And now you know the words.

[She puts her head on ALICE'S *other shoulder.]*

Just sing it through to *me*. I'm getting sleepy too.

[Both queens fall fast asleep and snore loudly.]

ALICE: What *am* I to do? Take care of two Queens asleep at once? Do wake up, you heavy things!

[All lights go out, leaving a mysterious glow on ALICE *and the queens.]*

WHITE RABBIT:

[Blows trumpet off stage.]

	The trial's beginning!
ALICE:	What trial is it?
WHITE RABBIT:	Who stole the tarts.
ALICE:	I ate a tart.
WHITE RABBIT:	You've got to be tried.
ALICE:	I don't want to be tried.
WHITE RABBIT:	You've got to be tried.
ALICE:	I won't be tried—I won't-I won't!

Scene Two – The Court of Hearts

Is a court room suggesting playing cards. The jurymen are all kinds of creatures. The KING and QUEEN OF HEARTS are seated on the throne. The KNAVE is before them in chains. The WHITE RABBIT has a trumpet in one hand, and a scroll of parchment in the other. In the middle of the court stands a table with a large dish of tarts upon it.

WHITE RABBIT:

[Blows three blasts on his trumpet.]

Silence in the court!

ALICE:

[Watches jurymen writing busily on their slates.]

What are they doing? They can't have anything to put down yet, before the trial's begun.

KNAVE: They're putting down their names for fear they should forget them before the end of the trial.

ALICE: Stupid things!

WHITE RABBIT: Silence in the court!

JURORS:

[Write in chorus.]

Stupid things!

ONE JUROR: How do you spell stupid?

ALICE: A nice muddle their slates will be in before the trial's over.

QUEEN: There's a pencil squeaking. Cut it down!

JURORS:

[*In chorus as they write.*]

Squeaking—

KING:

[*Wears a crown over his wig; puts on his spectacles as he says.*]

Herald, read the accusation!

WHITE **R**ABBIT:

[*Blows three blasts on his trumpet, unrolls parchment scroll and reads to music.*]

The Queen of Hearts, she made some tarts,
All on a summer day;
The Knave of Hearts, he stole those tarts,
And took them quite away!

KING: Consider your verdict!

WHITE **R**ABBIT: Not yet, not yet; there's a great deal to come before that.

KING: Call the first witness.

WHITE **R**ABBIT: First witness!

HATTER:

[*Comes in with a teacup in one hand and a piece of bread and butter in the other.*]

I beg your pardon, your Majesty, for bringing these in, but I hadn't quite finished my tea when I was sent for.

KING: You ought to have finished; when did you begin?

HATTER:

[*Looks at the* **M**ARCH **H**ARE, *who follows him arm-in-arm with the* **D**ORMOUSE.]

Fourteenth of March, I *think* it was.

MARCH **H**ARE: Fifteenth.

DORMOUSE:	Sixteenth.
KING:	Write that down.
JURY:	Fourteen, fifteen, sixteen—forty-five. Reduce that to shillings—
KING:	Take off your hat.
HATTER:	It isn't mine.
KING:	Stolen!
JURY:	Stolen!
HATTER:	I keep them to sell. I've none of my own. I'm a hatter.

QUEEN OF HEARTS:

[Puts on her spectacles and stares at HATTER, *who fidgets uncomfortably.]*

KING:	Give your evidence and don't be nervous, or I'll have you executed on the spot.

[The HATTER *continues to shift nervously from one foot to the other, looks uneasily at the* QUEEN, *trembles so that he shakes off both of his shoes, and in his confusion bites a large piece out of his teacup instead of the bread and butter.]*

HATTER:	I'm a poor man, your Majesty, and I hadn't but just begun my tea—not above a week or so—and what with the bread and butter getting so thin—and the twinkling of the tea—
KING:	The twinkling of *what?*
HATTER:	It began with the tea.
KING:	Of course twinkling begins with a T. Do you take me for a dunce? Go on!
HATTER:	I'm a poor man and most things twinkled after that—only the March Hare said—
MARCH HARE:	I didn't!
HATTER:	You did.

MARCH HARE: I deny it.

KING: He denies it; leave out that part.

QUEEN: But what did the Dormouse say?

HATTER: That I can't remember.

KING: You *must* remember or I'll have you executed.

HATTER:

[Drops teacup and bread and butter and goes down on one knee.]

I'm a poor man, your Majesty.

KING: If that's all you know about it you may stand down.

HATTER: I can't go no lower; I'm on the floor as it is.

KING: Then you may sit down.

HATTER: I'd rather finish my tea.

KING: You may go.

[The HATTER goes out hurriedly, leaving one of his shoes behind.]

QUEEN:

[Nonchalantly to an officer.]

And just take his head off outside.

[But the HATTER was out of sight before the officer could get to the door.]

KING: Call the next witness!

WHITE RABBIT: Next witness!

[The DUCHESS enters with a pepper pot, which she shakes about. Everybody begins to sneeze. MARCH HARE sneezes and rushes out.]

KING: Give your evidence!

DUCHESS: Shan't!

WHITE RABBIT: Your Majesty must cross-examine *this* witness.

KING: Well, if I must, I must. What does your cook say tarts are made of?

DUCHESS: Pepper.

[*The* DUCHESS *shakes the pot and the court sneezes.*]

DORMOUSE: Treacle!

[*The* DUCHESS *shakes the pot at him. He sneezes for the first time.*]

QUEEN: Collar the Dormouse! Behead the Dormouse! Turn that Dormouse out of court! Suppress him! Pinch him! Off with his whiskers!

[*The whole court is in confusion, turning the* DORMOUSE *out, and while it is settling down again the* DUCHESS *disappears.*]

WHITE RABBIT: The Duchess!

COURT: She's gone—she's gone.

KING: Never mind!

[*In a low tone to the* QUEEN.]

          Really, my dear, *you* must cross-examine the next witness. It quite makes my forehead ache! Call the next witness!

WHITE RABBIT:

[*Fumbles with the parchment, then cries in a shrill little voice.*]

          Alice!

ALICE: Here!

KING: What do you know about this business?

ALICE: Nothing whatever.

KING:

[*To the jury.*]

          That's very important.

WHITE RABBIT: Unimportant, your Majesty means, of course.

KING: Unimportant, of course I meant. Important—un-important—unimportant—important. Consider your verdict!

[Some of the jury write "important" and some write "unimportant."]

WHITE RABBIT: There's more evidence to come yet, please your Majesty; this paper has just been picked up.

QUEEN: What's in it?

WHITE RABBIT:

[Fumbles with a huge envelope.]

I haven't opened it yet, but it seems to be a letter, written by the prisoner to—to somebody.

KING: It must have been that unless it was written to nobody, which isn't usual, you know.

ALICE: Who is it directed to?

WHITE RABBIT: It isn't directed at all; in fact, there's nothing written on the *outside*.

[Takes out a tiny piece of paper.]

It isn't a letter at all; it's a set of verses.

QUEEN: Are they in the prisoner's handwriting?

[The jury brightens up.]

WHITE RABBIT:

[Looks at the KNAVE'S *hand.* KNAVE *hides his hand; the chains rattle.]*

No, they're not, and that's the queerest thing about it.

[The jury looks puzzled.]

KING: He must have imitated somebody else's hand!

KNAVE: Please, your Majesty, I didn't write it and they can't prove I did; there's no name signed at the end.

KING: If you didn't sign it that only makes the matter worse. You *must* have meant some mischief, or else you'd have signed your name like an honest man.

[*At this there is a general clapping of hands.*]

QUEEN: That *proves* his guilt.

ALICE: It proves nothing of the sort! Why, you don't even know what they're about.

KING: Read them!

WHITE RABBIT: [*Puts on his monocle.*]

Where shall I begin, please your Majesty?

KING: Begin at the beginning and go on till you come to the end, then stop.

WHITE RABBIT:

"They told me you had been to her,
And mentioned me to him;
She gave me a good character,
But said I could not swim.

"I gave her one, they gave him two,
You gave us three or more;
They all returned from him to you,
Though they were mine before.

"My notion was that you had been
(Before she had this fit)
An obstacle that came between
Him, and ourselves, and it.

"Don't let him know she liked him best,
For this must ever be
A secret, kept from all the rest,
Between yourself and me."

KING: That's the most important piece of evidence we've heard yet; so now let the jury—

ALICE: If anyone of them can explain it, I'll give him sixpence. I don't believe there's an atom of meaning in it.

JURY:	She doesn't believe there's an atom of meaning in it.
KING:	If there's no meaning in it, that saves a world of trouble, you know, as we needn't try to find any. And yet I don't know.

[Spreads out the verses on his knee and studies them.]

I seem to see some meaning after all. "Said I could not swim." You can't swim, can you?

KNAVE:

[Shakes his head sadly and points to his suit.]

Do I look like it?

KING: All right, so far; "We know it to be true," that's the jury, of course; "I gave her one, they gave him two" why that must be what he did with the tarts, you know—

ALICE: But it goes on "they all returned from *him* to *you*."

KING:

[Triumphantly pointing to the tarts.]

Why, there they are! Nothing can be clearer than that. Then again, "before she had this fit," you never had fits, my dear, I think?

QUEEN: Never!

KING: Then the words don't *fit* you.

[There is dead silence, while the KING looks around at the court with a smile.]

KING: It's a pun!

[Everybody laughs. Music.]

KING: Let the jury consider their verdict.

QUEEN: No, no! Sentence first—verdict afterwards.

ALICE: Stuff and nonsense!

QUEEN:

[Furiously.]

Hold your tongue!

ALICE: I won't!

QUEEN: Off with her head!

ALICE: Who cares for you?

QUEEN: Cut it off!

ALICE: You're nothing but a pack of cards!

[As lights go out and curtain falls all the characters hold their positions as if petrified.]

— CURTAIN —

Scene Three – Alice's Home

[The curtain rises to show Alice *still asleep in the armchair, the fire in the grate suffusing her with its glow.]*

CARROLL: Wake up, Alice, it is time for tea.

[Off stage the characters repeat their most characteristic lines, "Off with her head," "Consider your verdict," "Oh! my fur and whiskers"; the Duchess *sneezes, the cat cries,[Pg 133] as if the characters were fading away into the pack of real playing cards which shower through the mirror all over* Alice*. There is music.]*

ALICE: *[Wakes, rises, and looks about in surprise and wonderment.]*

          Why——it was a dream!

— The End —

Made in the USA
Monee, IL
07 July 2026

56550023R00052